To Mungo Taylor who would never be naughty like Mr Davies

First published 1996
by Walker Books Ltd, 87 Vauxhall Walk
London SE11 5HJ

This edition published 1997

2 4 6 8 10 9 7 5 3 1

© 1996 Charlotte Voake

Printed in Hong Kong

British Library Cataloguing in Publication Data
A catalogue record for this book is available from the British Library.

ISBN 0-7445-5237-0

THIS WALKER BOOK BELONGS TO:

_____

_____

_____

_____

Mr Davies
and the Baby

Charlotte
Voake

WALKER BOOKS
AND SUBSIDIARIES
LONDON • BOSTON • SYDNEY

Once upon a time there was a little dog
called Mr Davies. All day long
he stayed in his garden.

He sniffed the smells and dug
holes in the flower beds.

He ate his meals, and when it rained
he slept in his kennel.

Next door to Mr Davies lived a baby.

Every single day, the baby
and his mother went
out for a walk.

"Hello, Mr Davies," the baby's mother said.
The baby clapped his hands and laughed
and Mr Davies wagged his tail.
Mr Davies watched them go down
the road and wished he could
go with them.

Then one day,
Mr Davies
found he could
squeeze right
under the gate,
and he came
out to meet
the baby.

The baby was very excited.
So was Mr Davies,
and he jumped about
and wagged his tail.
"Nice dog," said
the baby's mother.
"Now go home,
Mr Davies."

But Mr Davies was much too excited to listen.
He just wagged his tail harder
and followed them
down the road.

Mr Davies was very good
until he saw some ducks.

"Mr Davies, come here!"
shouted the baby's mother.

The next day Mr Davies
went for a walk
with the baby again.
But this time
he chased
a cat.

And the next day Mr Davies
saw a man on a bicycle
and chased him
up the road.

People asked the baby's mother, "Is this your dog?"
"No, he is not," she said.

One day the baby's mother went next door.

"Please could you stop Mr Davies
getting out of the garden?" she asked.

The next day Mr Davies ran to meet the baby

and the baby held out his arms...

But just as Mr Davies got to the gate he came
to a sudden STOP.

Poor Mr Davies had been tied to his kennel!

He barked and barked but he could not get free.

The baby and his mother set off down
the road. Soon they couldn't hear
Mr Davies barking any more.
The baby was sad.
Even the baby's mother
was sorry that Mr Davies
had been tied up.

It was very quiet.

Then suddenly they heard
a SMASHING
and a BANGING
and a happy BARKING

coming towards them.

It was Mr Davies…

and he was bringing his kennel with him!

The very next day the baby
and his mother bought Mr Davies
a beautiful lead.

Now he goes walking with them
every day, and everyone
is happy,

even the ducks!

MORE WALKER PAPERBACKS
For You to Enjoy

Also by Charlotte Voake

MRS GOOSE'S BABY

Shortlisted for the Best Book for Babies Award
There's something very strange about Mrs Goose's baby – but her
mother love is so great that she alone cannot see what it is!
"An ideal picture book for the youngest child." *The Good Book Guide*
0-7445-4791-1   £4.99

TOM'S CAT

There are all sorts of noises around the house –
but which, if any, is coming from Tom's cat?
"Among my favourites ... ingenious and very funny."
Quentin Blake, The Independent
0-7445-5272-9   £4.99

AMY SAID

written by Martin Waddell
"A triumph… Text and pictures work in harness as the children
provoke one another to ever worsening behaviour. Understatement
and lightness of touch couldn't find better exposition."
The Times Educational Supplement
0-7445-5227-3   £4.99

Walker Paperbacks are available from most booksellers, or by post from B.B.C.S., P.O. Box 941, Hull, North Humberside HU1 3YQ
24 hour telephone credit card line 01482 224626
To order, send: Title, author, ISBN number and price for each book ordered, your full name and address,
cheque or postal order payable to BBCS for the total amount and allow the following for postage and packing:
UK and BFPO: £1.00 for the first book, and 50p for each additional book to a maximum of £3.50.
Overseas and Eire: £2.00 for the first book, £1.00 for the second and 50p for each additional book.
Prices and availability are subject to change without notice.